W9-BDP-416

PUFFIN BOOKS
TILL THE CLOUDS ROLL BY

Born in Kasauli in 1934, Ruskin Bond grew up in Jamnagar, Dehradun, New Delhi and Simla. His first novel, *The Room on the Roof*, written when he was seventeen, received the John Llewellyn Rhys Memorial Prize in 1957. Since then he has written over 500 short stories, essays and novellas and more than forty books for children.

He received the Sahitya Akademi Award for English writing in India in 1992, the Padma Shri in 1999 and the Padma Bhushan in 2014. He lives in Landour, Mussoorie, with his extended family.

Also in Puffin by Ruskin Bond

Getting Granny's Glasses

Earthquake

The Cherry Tree

The Eyes of the Eagle

Dust on the Mountain

Cricket for the Crocodile

Puffin Classics: The Room on the Roof

Puffin Classics: Vagrants in the Valley

The Room of Many Colours: A Treasury of Stories for Children

Panther's Moon and Other Stories

The Hidden Pool

The Parrot Who Wouldn't Talk and Other Stories

Mr Oliver's Diary

Escape from Java and Other Tales of Danger

Crazy Times with Uncle Ken

Rusty: The Boy from the Hills

Rusty Runs Away

Rusty and the Leopard

Rusty Goes to London

Rusty Comes Home

Rusty and the Magic Mountain

The Puffin Book of Classic School Stories

The Puffin Good Reading Guide for Children

The Kashmiri Storyteller

Hip-Hop Nature Boy and Other Poems

The Adventures of Rusty: Collected Stories

Thick as Thieves: Tales of Friendship

Uncles, Aunts and Elephants: Tales from Your Favourite Storyteller

Ranji's Wonderful Bat and Other Stories

Whispers in the Dark: A Book of Spooks

The Tree Lover

The Day Grandfather Tickled a Tiger

Looking for the Rainbow

RUSKIN BOND

TILL THE Clouds ROLL BY

Beginning again

Illustrations by Mihir Joglekar

PUFFIN BOOKS

An imprint of Penguin Random House

PUFFIN BOOKS

USA | Canada | UK | Ireland | Australia
New Zealand | India | South Africa | China

Puffin Books is part of the Penguin Random House group of companies
whose addresses can be found at global.penguinrandomhouse.com

Published by Penguin Random House India Pvt. Ltd.
4th Floor, Capital Tower 1, MG Road,
Gurugram 122 002, Haryana, India

Penguin
Random House
India

First published in Puffin Books by Penguin Random House India 2017

Text copyright © Ruskin Bond 2017
Illustrations copyright © Mihir Joglekar 2017

10 9 8 7 6 5 4 3 2

The views and opinions expressed in this book are the author's own and the
facts are as reported by him, which have been verified to the extent possible,
and the publishers are not in any way liable for the same.

ISBN 9780143442127

Typeset in Baskerville
Book design and layout by Devangana Dash
Printed at Replika Press Pvt. Ltd, India

www.penguin.co.in

CONTENTS

PREFACE

This little story, true in every respect, has been written as a sequel to *Looking for the Rainbow,* which was so well received by readers of all ages.

Looking for the Rainbow told the story of the two years I spent with my father in New Delhi and Simla, after my parents' separation. His sudden death precipitated me into a different and unfamiliar world.

The transition from an English father to a Punjabi stepfather demanded an adjustment that was far from easy for a ten-year-old boy who had just lost his father. When I came down to Dehradun from my hill school, it was to a home that had yet to become a home. This is the story of that winter holiday over seventy years ago. To me it seems like yesterday.

If I made the adjustment, it was partly because of one or two unlikely friendships and partly because of a streak of independence in my nature, which helped define me as an individual in my own right.

Most of us grow in our teens or twenties. I think I grew up when I was ten.

Ruskin Bond
Landour, Mussoorie
September 2017

1

A HOUSE WITH LICHEE TREES

Looking back across the years, I seem to have spent a large part of my boyhood on trains—the small train taking me up to Simla and my boarding school; the overnight train to Dehradun, to my mother's and stepfather's home; or trains along the coast, trains across the desert, trains through field and forest. And sitting on railway platforms, waiting for trains to arrive or depart. No wonder so many of my earlier stories are set in trains or on railway platforms.

Well, this is a new story about my life, of when I was ten and coming 'home' to Dehra for my winter holidays, a few months after my father had been taken from me by Death's dark angel.

And here's the train, chugging through a gap in the foothills, the green-and-gold steam engine giving out a shrill whistle as it plunges into the forest, warning the jungle folk of its approach. The deer and the wild boars scatter, but an elephant takes up the challenge, trumpeting a response from the shallows of the little Suswa River. The train rumbles over a bridge and a small boy looks out of a carriage window, at the clear waters of the stream and the little wayside station that stands beside it.

The train slows down—there's a rise in the gradient—then picks up speed again and emerges from the forest, rushing past small villages and fields of rice and waving wheat and yellow mustard. A village boy sees the boy at the window and waves to him, and the boy in the train waves back. A bond has been created—if only for a moment in time, but a moment captured forever.

The train moves on, through the rolling pastures of the Doon. Cows graze; buffaloes wallow in ponds; herons alight on the buffaloes. I am the boy at the window; a sturdy boy, but a little pensive, a little gloomy, wondering what the future has in store for me. I haven't seen my mother for over two years. My stepfather I saw only once, in his photo studio, when my mother took me there to be photographed. I remember him only as a thin man behind a mounted camera, and that he had a thin moustache. This was a year or two before my parents separated— before I went to stay with my father in Delhi.

The engine slows down again. We are approaching the Dehradun station, the end of the line. Will somebody be there to meet me? My mother perhaps, and my young brother. Possibly even my stepfather, Mr Hari.

There are other boys on the train. They tumble out on to the small platform to be greeted by

fond parents. Hugs and kisses abound; I am the last to get down from the compartment. I look up and down the platform. There are no familiar faces. Perhaps they have sent someone for me. So I wait. I wait for the crowd to thin out, for the clamour to subside. A coolie stands at my elbow, eager to pick up my trunk and bedding roll and earn half a rupee. I ask him to wait. 'Somebody will be coming,' I say.

But no one comes.

*

Half an hour passed, and I was sitting alone on an empty platform. I couldn't remain there all day. There was only one thing to do—engage a tonga and go to Granny's house, on Old Survey Road. I had the number of the house and a vague idea of the direction in which it lay. I didn't have any other address.

The patient coolie loaded my trunk and bedding roll on to a tonga, and I paid him with the last of my travel money. If there was no one at Granny's house, who would pay for the tonga? And to make matters worse, I hadn't had any breakfast!

Clip-clop, the tonga pony went trotting through the town, the flimsy carriage rattling and swaying along. I was in the front seat, beside the driver. The pony raised its tail and passed wind. Welcome to Dehra!

Dehradun, the little town famous for its lichee trees. Yes, there they were, surrounding almost every bungalow; neatly spaced out, unlike the tall, spreading mango trees that overlooked them.

We bumped along for almost half an hour, then came to a gate with the number '6' painted on it. I recognized the old railway-style bungalow (built by my grandfather on his retirement from the railways) and the big jackfruit tree growing against the veranda. The gate was open and we rattled up to the porch.

No one seemed to be home.

'Granny, Granny!' I called. 'Is anyone home?'

All was still. Then, a sudden squawk, and I was almost deafened by a large parrot shrieking at me from its perch above a hanging basket.

'Ring the bell, ring the bell!' it screeched. It had obviously been trained to say this to unwary callers.

I found the bell and rang it.

Presently the front door opened and my granny stepped out.

She was a large, heavily built woman, with white hair and a florid complexion. She stood wearing carpet slippers and a faded red dressing gown.

'Ruskin!' she exclaimed. 'What are you doing here?'

'I'm home for my holidays, Granny. Where's Mummy?'

'Didn't she meet you?'

'There was no one at the station. I took a tonga and came straight here.'

'They don't live here. Your mother and—and the rest of them—live in Dalanwala. It's strange they didn't receive you. I'd better take you there.'

But she changed her mind when she saw the tonga pony. It was a white pony—and Granny would *never* get on a tonga with a white pony. Not since a runaway one had deposited her and the tonga and the tonga driver in one of the local canals.

So she paid the driver his fare and gave him careful instructions as to how to find my mother's and stepfather's house.

'You can't miss it,' she told me. 'It's surrounded by lichee trees.'

'All the houses are surrounded by lichee trees,' I said.

And so they were. But we finally found the right one, and we were welcomed—not by my mother and stepfather, but by a cook-cum-bearer called Mela Ram, who was surprised to see me.

Mela Ram was a young man from the hills, who had taken up a job at my stepfather's house after a poor monsoon had dried up his fields.

'They thought you were coming tomorrow,' he said. 'They are out hunting—shikar—and won't be back till evening. But come, I have lunch ready for you.'

Having missed breakfast, I was only too ready for lunch, and I wolfed down everything he served me—dal and rice and aloo gobi—without realizing that I was probably eating his lunch too.

Afterwards, while unpacking in the bedroom, I encountered three toddlers playing with a train set.

'One is your real brother,' said Mela Ram, indicating the boy who looked a bit like me. 'The second is your half-brother. And the third is your half-brother's other brother.'

Mela Ram seemed to be as confused as I was; but everything got sorted out in time.

2

WHERE HAVE ALL THE TIGERS GONE?

My mother and stepfather returned late at night, after we had all fallen asleep, and I did not see them until the following morning. As they had slept late, it was almost noon before my mother came into the large bedroom that I was sharing with my brothers, gave me a hug and a kiss and wanted to know why I had arrived a day early! Had there been a change of date, and why hadn't the school informed her? I did not know of any changes—I had been put on the train with several other boys, and here I was, home and dry.

My stepfather, Mr Hari, gave me a perfunctory handshake and promised to take me on his next hunting foray into the jungle. He then got into his Ford V8 and drove off to his automobile workshop. The photo studio had been given to Mr Hari at the time of his first marriage, to a Hindu lady. But his heart wasn't really in photography; he wanted to buy and sell cars, fast ones preferably.

For several days I was left to my own devices. Missing my father, I went for long, lonely walks along the little lanes around Dalanwala, the area where we were living. I missed his companionship, the tone of his voice, the feel of his hands; I missed his stamp collection and the old gramophone, and presumed these were still in Calcutta, where he had died. I missed my school friends too, but hopefully would see them again when the winter holidays were over.

And so, hands in the pockets of my grey flannel shorts, I explored the roads and byways of Dehra. When my mother gave me pocket money, I went to the cinema. And I discovered a little bookshop where I bought comic papers and film magazines. There were some books at home—mostly 'Westerns', my stepfather's favourite reading—and I went through the works of Max Brand, Luke Short and Zane Grey. Lots of gunplay and wild rides across the 'mesa' (whatever that may have been), the tales forgotten the day they were finished. There was also a copy of *Little Women*, which my mother must have kept from her schooldays. Although this was considered a girl's book, I thoroughly enjoyed it. Quite a reader by now, I was up for reading anything that came my way.

One day, out of sheer boredom, I put the three small boys—brother, half-brother and stepbrother—in a pram and took them for a long ride. Down the road, past the house and down to the little riverbed that separated the town from the jungle. Most of the riverbed was dry, full of boulders, but a thin stream ran through it. We were paddling about in the shallow waters,

19

having a great time, when I noticed an elephant standing on the other bank of the riverbed.

Elephants are friendly enough when their mahouts (or keepers) are with them, but this one looked like a wild elephant, separated from its herd.

'Hathi, hathi!' called the children, pointing towards the tusker.

The elephant began to walk into the riverbed, probably in search of water, and I thought it prudent to head for home. I bundled the three brothers into the pram, struggled to climb up the stony bank and did not stop pushing until we had reached the pukka road. Looking back, I saw that the elephant was now in the middle of the riverbed. It was unlikely that it would enter a residential area, but I did not wait to discover its intentions. Helter-skelter, the pram, the children and I rattled along the narrow road until we arrived safely at our gate.

After that, they demanded a pram ride every day, but I passed this treat on to Mela Ram. My brother, William, was three. Harold, my half-brother, was two. The eldest, Nandu, was four years old. He was my stepfather's son by his first wife, who lived over a shop in the bazaar. The boy had been sent over to our place so that he could get to know his brothers. I had never seen his mother, but I was to encounter that mysterious lady before my holidays were over.

Meanwhile, there was the big shikar safari.

My mother and Mr Hari had planned to spend a week in the jungle, staying in a forest rest house, and I was invited to accompany them. There would be others in the party—a couple of my stepfather's employers from his photo studio (they had guns of their own), a hired cook and a boy assistant to help with the dishwashing and other jobs. The children would, as usual, be left behind with Mela Ram.

At first I was reluctant to join them. I was only ten, and guns were rather frightening. And I had a vivid imagination.

*

We set off in two jeeps and, after an hour's drive along a bumpy forest road, arrived at a fairly large forest bungalow situated in a clearing.

The day was ending, and no one was interested in going out to look for a tiger by the moonlight. The tiger would definitely have the advantage. My mother and stepfather settled down to a round of their favourite drink—rum and soda water—while the rest of the company sang and danced round a campfire, thus ensuring that the jungle folk were made aware of their presence. I joined the cook and his assistant, Mohan, in their preparation of dinner.

The next morning, two tame elephants were engaged, and I found myself on one of them, sharing a precarious howdah with a couple of shikaris. My mother and Mr Hari were perched on the other elephant, guns at the ready.

Into the jungle we sallied, making enough noise to warn Shere Khan the tiger, Bagheera the panther, Baloo the bear and all their friends and companions of our coming. Still, the odd jungle creature did manage to stray into our path. Junglefowl flew off in various directions, and one or two were brought down. There was a deafening blast from one of the guns beside me, and a spotted deer rolled over in the grass.

In its last throes, the wounded deer lay there kicking and convulsing, and this upset our elephant, who backed away, leaving the narrow track. The branch of a tree caught me around the chest and almost swept me off the howdah. It took the mahout several minutes to get the elephant under control. By then I was flat on my back between the two shikaris.

'Are you all right, Ruskin?' called my mother from her elephant.

'No!' I shouted back. 'I want to get off!'

I was just as upset as that sensitive elephant and was glad to be escorted back to the rest house, where the cook kindly applied mustard oil to my bruised chest.

I did not accompany the hunting party after that. The image of the dying deer haunted me— and still does, today.

*

But that week in the jungle was not without its rewards.

The following day, when the hunting party headed for the jungle, I had the rest house to myself—except for Mohan, the boy assistant, who had been left in charge of the kitchen.

Exploring the old bungalow, I discovered a storeroom at the rear—a room full of old and broken furniture: a settee with the stuffing coming out, a bed with broken springs, a cupboard with a missing door. The remaining door swung open at my touch to reveal a treasure trove of books—books that were in good condition because they hadn't been touched for years, the collection of some bygone forest officer perhaps.

Here I found enough reading to keep me occupied for the rest of the week. Here I discovered the ghost stories of M.R. James, that master of the supernatural tale, scholarly and convincing. Here I discovered an early

P.G. Wodehouse novel, *Love among the Chickens*, featuring Ukridge, that happy optimist, who was to become my favourite Wodehouse character. Ukridge always addresses everyone as 'old horse'—'And how are you, old horse?' or 'Lend me a fiver, old horse!'—and for several months I found myself addressing friends and families in the same manner, until one day, back in school, I addressed my headmaster as 'old horse' and received a caning for my pains.

In the forest bungalow I also discovered Agatha Christie's first Poirot novel, *The Mysterious Affair at Styles*, John Buchan's spy thriller *The Thirty-Nine Steps* and the short stories of O. Henry and W.W. Jacobs. There were some children's books in that cupboard too—and I have to confess that I read very few children's books as a boy. I had gone straight from comic papers to adult fiction!

The front veranda of the bungalow had a very comfortable armchair, and I spent most of the day stretched out in it with one of those books for company. Instead of becoming a great shikari, as my mother and stepfather might have wished, I had become an incurable bookworm, and was to remain one for the rest of my life.

Mohan would bring me bread and butter and a glass of hot tea, and I was quite content with this spartan lunch. The cook and the food baskets would go along with the shikar party, who would be enjoying mutton koftas and pilau rice whenever they tired of following an elusive tiger. But I was having an adventure of my own.

The only interruption came late one afternoon when the silence was broken by screams for help emanating from the kitchen.

Had Mohan been seized by a man-eating tiger, or possibly a ravenous python?

I rushed to his assistance. I may have been a bookish boy, but I was no coward.

Mohan, moving around barefoot, had been stung by a scorpion and was in considerable pain.

I remembered having read something about vinegar being an antidote for scorpion sting and various other insect bites, and I located a bottle on the kitchen shelf. Did he have to drink the stuff or did I need to apply it? The latter, of course! So I soaked my handkerchief in vinegar and doused his swollen ankle. It must have been worse than the scorpion sting because Mohan kept yelling. So I made him lie down in the armchair in the veranda, and covered him with a blanket.

After some time, the pain began to subside, but he grew feverish. He kept asking for his mother. I wasn't much of a substitute, but I went indoors and found my mother's aspirin bottle— aspirin was just about the only available pain medication in those days—and made Mohan swallow a couple. I had done my best. Boy Scouts forever!

Towards evening the shikar party returned, still without a tiger, and Mohan was put in one of the jeeps and driven back to Dehra and his mother. He was up and about a couple of days later. Maybe the vinegar had helped.

*

Tigerless, the expedition petered out the following day.

'Where have all the tigers gone?' grumbled Mr Hari.

'Jim Corbett shot the last one,' I said, but my joke was not appreciated.

The shikar party decided to make one last rumble through the jungle in search of the fabled tiger. It was literally a rumble, because Mr Hari had engaged some thirty to forty villagers from across the river to 'beat' the jungle—that is, to advance in a line through the forest, beating drums, or kerosene tins, and blowing on horns, or home-made trumpets, in a bid to drive the forest creatures out of their lairs and into the open.

This they succeeded in doing, but in the wrong direction.

While the hunters waited for their quarry at the edge of the forest, the villagers—confused by the trumpeting of the elephants—took another route, in effect driving the animals to safety, and in the direction of the rest house.

I was sitting in the veranda, a book on my knee, when I heard a lot of grunting and squealing. I looked up to see a number of wild boars streaming across the clearing in front of me! They emerged from one side of the jungle and disappeared into the thickets on the other side.

Now they were followed by a herd of deer— beautiful spotted chital, and then handsome, tall sambar. All emerging from the trees, moving swiftly across the clearing and making their way into the forest.

Peacocks and junglefowl, also disturbed by the village orchestra, flew across the clearing, exchanging sal for shisham.

Fascinated by this sudden appearance of birds and beasts, I remained sitting in my armchair—not in the least alarmed—because it was obvious that the animals were intent on getting as far away from humans as possible.

And presently I was rewarded with the sight of a lithe and sinewy leopard slinking past the bungalow. It may have been looking out for its own safety or it may have been following the deer, but there it was—all black and gold in the late afternoon sun.

And then it vanished into the dense green foliage.

Hours later, the hunters returned, grumpy and empty-handed except for an unfortunate barking deer.

'I saw a leopard while you were away,' I told my mother and stepfather.

They were not impressed.

'He's making it up,' said Mr Hari.

'Well, he does have a vivid imagination,' said my mother. 'It must be all those books he's been reading.'

I did not argue with them. You don't argue with adults who have made up their minds about you.

The tiger had eluded them, but I had seen a leopard. So I had achieved a small victory.

3

THE FIRST LADY SHOPKEEPER

Back in Dehra, with my siblings for company, life became rather monotonous. My mother and Mr Hari went to their parties, and I stayed at home with whatever books I could accumulate. Occasionally I accompanied Mela Ram to the sabzi mandi (vegetable market), where the colourful stalls were piled high with fruit from all over the country—papayas, oranges, lemons, bananas, pears, guavas, custard apples, grapefruit, pineapples, pomegranates . . . Just looking at them gave me a thrill. I remembered my father telling me that there was no country in the world so rich in the variety of its fruit as India—I could see that this was true. And the summer fruits had yet to come!

While Mela Ram filled his shopping basket with vegetables, I sank my teeth into a juicy pear or guava and advised him on its quality. He knew better than me, of course, and was quick to tell the difference between a fresh apple and one that had been made to look fresh.

One day, he set off for the market with the pram and Nandu in it.

'His mother has sent for him,' he said. 'So I shall deliver him on my way to the mandi.'

'I'll come with you,' I said.

'She may not like that. She blames your mother for a lot of things.'

'And does she blame Mr Hari?'

'He is a weak man—but he has given her the shop. Bibiji is the town's first lady shopkeeper!'

I was curious to see my stepfather's first wife, who ran a little provisions store in the heart of the bazaar.

'I'll stay out of sight,' I said. 'I'll wait near the petrol station while you drop off Nandu.'

Nandu was duly delivered, and he went scampering off into the inner regions of his mother's shop, the Royal Provision Store. I expected to see a frail, delicate, dignified woman behind the counter, but Bibiji turned out to be a robust, solidly built woman in her mid-thirties. She was ruddy-faced and had strong arms. Mela Ram had told me that she could lift sacks of wheat or rice without any fuss and, looking at her now, I could well believe it. I had been staring at her for some time when she looked up, saw me from across the road, asked a question of Mela Ram and then beckoned me to come over.

When I reached the shopfront, she gave me a long, hard look and said, 'So you are Bond ka beta!' Then she offered me a seat on the other side of the counter. Mela Ram went off to fetch tea from a nearby dhaba.

Bibiji could not speak English and my Hindi was elementary, but we managed a conversation of sorts. She said she had seen my father once, when he had come to fetch me, and that he had seemed a very polite but reserved sort of man. She did not have anything nice to say about her husband or my mother, and that was understandable.

After some time, a customer came in and made a few purchases and asked for a bill. Bibiji had some difficulty making out a cash memo, and I realized that she hadn't been to a proper school. So I took the bill pad from her, listed the purchases and their prices and totalled it all up. This pleased her tremendously.

Most of the items she sold were household provisions—an assortment of lentils, rice, wheat flour, salt, ghee, potatoes, onions, chillies. All the necessities of life.

When we had finished our tea, she asked me to draft a letter for her, ordering some tins of pickle, and this too I did to her satisfaction. She told Mela Ram to bring me again, and I walked home with mixed feelings.

I had made a friend of Bibiji, but had I, in some way, been deceitful towards my mother and stepfather? Had I gone over to the other side? I mentioned my visit to my mother, but she did not seem concerned. Another baby was on the way, and she obviously had other things to think about.

*

The baby—another boy—arrived on time, and so did Dehra's first snowfall of the century.

It was about five in the evening when the snow came down, large clinging flakes that soon covered the roof, the trees and the bushes with a blanket of pure white. I had been loafing about on the road when it started and ran indoors, shouting, 'Mummy, Mummy, it's snowing outside!'

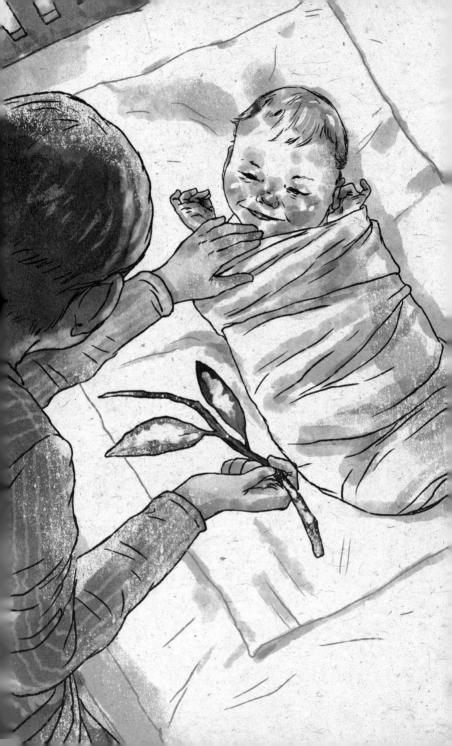

'I'm not in the mood for your silly jokes,' said my mother from her bed.

So I went outside again and broke a branch off one of the lichee trees. The leaves were dusted with snow. I took it inside and showed it to my mother, who said, 'Yes, that's snow all right. Your granny says it snowed when she got married— over forty years ago.'

Then I showed the snow-covered branch to the baby, though he wasn't impressed. But when I tickled him under the chin, he smiled.

The sun went down and the moon came up, and the snow-decked garden looked very pretty in the moonlight.

The next morning, Mela Ram and I made snowballs and flung them at passing cyclists and tongas. Later, when the sun came out, the snow melted too quickly and by noon, it had all gone.

4

THE MAKING OF FRIENDS

Having got to know Dehra by walking, or rather meandering, all around the town, I became more ambitious and wanted to explore its outskirts—the fields, the canals that fed them, the tea gardens, the forest glades. Over a month of my holidays had gone by, and another remained for exploration. And this became easier when Mela Ram brought home a second-hand bicycle.

My mother had given him the money to buy it, so that time would be saved on his expeditions to and from the bazaar. At first I would accompany him, sitting on the saddle or the crossbar. But once I had learnt to ride the thing, I took it over and cycled off on my own, sometimes taking the roads that led out of Dehra—to Delhi, or Saharanpur, or Rishikesh, or the foothills.

Of course I paid the occasional visit to Bibiji's little shop, and she made good use of my visits, getting me to make out bills or write letters or translate official notices, like tax demands. But she appreciated my help and rewarded me with samosas or pakoras obtained from the nearby dhaba. She liked talking to me too, and I would listen patiently to her grievances, directed mostly at my mother and stepfather. She could not pronounce 'Ruskin' properly, and always called me 'Rucksun', which I accepted as a Punjabi variant of my name.

She was a practical, unsentimental person, who was determined to make a success of her shop. I think she grew quite fond of me as time went on.

But time passed swiftly, having not much else to do, and my winter holidays were fast coming to an end.

Meanwhile, the bicycle took me further and further afield.

One day I stopped to rest by the Suswa, which came down in a stream from the Siwalik Hills, and there I noticed a youth sitting on the wall of a culvert, a fishing rod in his hands. He was gazing at the water, intent on catching a fish. I could not see any in the running water, but perhaps he could hypnotize one into coming up for the bait on his fishing line.

He looked up and saw me only when I was right beside him; we both recognized each other instantly. It was Mohan, the cook's assistant, who had been stung by a scorpion in the forest rest house!

'Catching a fish for dinner?' I asked in a bantering tone.

He nodded seriously. 'I'm using a special bait today—a small snail.'

'Well, good luck with it. Not working these days?'

'Last cook I worked for expired. So I'm taking a holiday. Another cook hires me next week.'

'So you're between jobs—between cooks.'

He nodded again, his hands being occupied with his rod and tackle, a simple home-made fishing rod. I joined him on the wall, and before long we were exchanging personal histories. We had one thing in common; we had both lost our fathers the previous year. His father had been killed in a road accident. A sudden illness had snatched mine away when I most needed him. But I had a home to come to and a school to return to. Whereas Mohan came from a poor family—his father, a domestic servant—and after his father's death, the boy had had to go out to earn a living for himself, his mother and his young brothers and sisters. They lived in a small room behind the railway station.

We sat there for almost an hour before Mohan caught anything. It was a still day, the leaves of the sal trees barely moving. Somewhere a peacock called. Then there was the whistle of an approaching engine, and we could see a passenger train coming down the incline from Dehra, chugging through open country and then disappearing into the sal forest.

'Have you been on the train?' I asked.

'Only as far as Hardwar. And then without a ticket. And you?'

'I will be on that train a little less than a month from now. Back to my boarding school in Simla for another nine months. But I'll return next winter. Will you still be here?'

'Probably.'

'Trying to catch a fish.'

Just then, he actually caught a fish. There was a tug on his line and a moment later, a small fish, about seven inches long, was flopping around on the grass. Mohan hadn't really expected to catch anything, but there it was—a little silver fish gleaming in the sunshine. He was overjoyed. You would think he'd just harpooned a whale!

'It's not very big,' I pointed out.

'Better a small fish than an empty dish,' came the reply. It sounded like one of Granny's proverbs.

I offered to take him home on the bicycle. So he put the fish in Mela Ram's shopping basket and we cycled back to town. Mohan did the pedalling, since he was older and stronger, while I perched on the handlebars, guarding his fish. He left me near the railway station after promising to meet me the following day. I cycled home to be scolded by my mother for making off with the bicycle just when it was needed by Mela Ram.

But Mela Ram didn't mind. He was quite happy to have been strolling around in the bazaar, chatting to his friends and keeping the memsahib waiting.

*

Mohan and I went to the pictures together. That day, I had enough pocket money for the both of us, and we cycled down to the old Filmistan cinema near the railway station. Mohan had found some part-time work during the day, so it had to be an evening show. When I'd be on my own, I would see English films at the little Odeon cinema, but to please Mohan, whose English was limited, I suggested a Hindi film. We saw *Tansen*, a biopic about the great singer who sang in Akbar's court. Tansen was played by the famous singer K.L. Saigal, and singing with him was the beautiful actress Khursheed.

Well, you'd have to be as old as me, or older, to remember that film—unless you've picked it up on late-night TV.

I can't say I enjoyed it, but it was good to sit there with Mohan and enjoy his enjoyment. He did not watch many films, and any picture was an experience for him. The songs were memorable, but the action dragged on interminably and I was glad when the interval came.

During the interval, we ate samosas and drank hot sweet tea. When we returned to our seats, I promptly fell asleep.

The following day, I went to see Granny. Perhaps I'd get some encouragement, some good advice from her. But she seemed preoccupied, taken up with her own problems.

When I told her I was hungry, she gave me two thick slices of bread and some butter.

'Don't you have any jam, Granny?'

Gooseberry
JAM

Granny had always disapproved of too many sweet things. But she hunted around in a cupboard and found a jar of gooseberry jam.

'Don't eat too much of it,' she warned. 'You'll get sick.'

But I slapped it on generously. Who cared about getting sick? Gooseberry jam forever!

'Do you have any books?' I asked.

She led me to the veranda at the back, where there was a shelf full of books. But they were mostly religious tracts and books of sermons. Not one to be discouraged, I rummaged through the contents and finally came upon some bound copies of *The Wide World Magazine*. I pounced on these and asked Granny if I could have them.

'Take them,' she said. 'They were your grandfather's. He liked reading about faraway places.'

I'd discovered books in the forest rest house, and now these old magazines in Granny's veranda. I was growing into a boy who looked for books in out-of-the-way places.

*

Granny was a rather stern person, not too fond of children. If she was fond of me, she did not show it; her rough exterior hid her concern for the family.

'How's your mother?' she asked one day.

'Oh, she's fine, Granny.'

'And your brothers?'

'They're just fine.'

'And I suppose you're fine too?'

'Yes, I'm doing fine, Granny. Back to school soon.'

'Well, remember to wash your hands regularly, and say your prayers every night.'

Now, these were two things that I seldom remembered to do, but I promised not to forget.

'And what do you want to be when you grow up?'

'A tap dancer,' I said, after giving it some thought.

'You've been watching too many films,' said Granny.

Too many films, too many books . . . was I just a dreamer?

'Now give the parrot a chilli and you can go home.'

I paid my respects to the parrot and took off.

5

FOLLOW THE RAINBOW

And so the holidays drew to a close, and my mother got down to the business of packing my trunk. I had grown a bit, and new khaki shorts and pants had to be tailored. The war was drawing to a close too, but khaki was still in fashion. It stood for discipline and order. On parade! Everyone had to look the same.

I wasn't really longing for early morning PT and other forms of regulation. The holidays hadn't been great, but better than I'd expected. I had gone into the jungle and discovered books—a real adventure!—and books would be with me for the rest of my life, whereas tigers, leopards and wild elephants would be confined to my dreams. And, quite by chance, I had made an odd mixture of friends—Mela Ram, Mohan,

even Bibiji! My stepfather hadn't taken much notice of me, and somehow that suited me; I was left alone. And now my mother was busy getting me ready for school.

'This blazer is much too small for you,' she observed.

'In school it will be called a bottom-freezer,' I said.

'And the buttons have fallen off all your shirts. And your pyjamas are torn. Don't you have a tie?'

'Left it in the jungle,' I said. 'A monkey made off with it. School ties look good on monkeys.'

The tailor worked overtime on my clothes while I set off on my bicycle to pay a last round of visits.

*

'Ring the bell, ring the bell!' screamed Granny's parrot.

Dutifully I rang the bell, but Granny did not come to the door. Instead the old gardener came up the veranda steps and told me Granny had gone to Bangalore to stay with her eldest daughter. He gave the parrot a green chilli and invited me to do the same. The parrot tried to bite my finger off. I don't think it liked small boys.

Next, I cycled off to the bazaar and paid my respects to Bibiji. She got me to make out yet more bills and presented me with a jar of mixed pickle.

'They don't allow pickles in my school,' I said. 'Our headmaster says they heat the blood! And that makes us break the rules.'

So she gave me a jar of guava jelly instead. 'This will cool the blood,' she said with one of her rare smiles.

*

No one had greeted me on the day of my arrival, but now almost everyone saw me off. Mr Hari drove us to the station in his Ford V8—my mother, the baby, my brothers and I—while Mela Ram followed on the bicycle. At Ambala I would change trains and join a party of boys from Delhi.

Slowly, the train drew out of Dehra's small station and up the gradient that led to the foothills. I remained at my window, watching the platform recede, the town slip away, the valley open up. The steam engine went chugging over the undulating land, and then the forest closed in and the engine let out a loud, penetrating whistle. In the distance, an elephant trumpeted a challenge. It had not yet lost its right to the forest.

Presently we were crossing the slender Suswa River and, looking upstream, I could clearly make out the little footbridge where Mohan had been fishing . . . And there he was now, perched above

the stream, rod in hand! I was sure it was Mohan. I waved frantically, but he did not see me. He was deep in concentration, determined to catch a fish. My heart went out to him. I wanted him to catch a fish, I willed him to catch a fish. Or perhaps I was willing a fish to be caught!

He looked up. Had he seen me, a boy waving from the window of a passing train? The engine picked up speed, and soon he was out of sight. The river ran one way and the train, the other.

And I resolved that the next winter, when the holidays came round again, I would find Mohan and we would go fishing together. Or was I just dreaming again . . .

Suddenly, a curtain of rain swept across the hills, and raindrops came in through the window, stinging my eyes. Spring was in the air. I remembered a record I used to play on my father's gramophone, and the words of the song came back to me:

Though April showers

May come your way,

They bring the flowers

That bloom in May . . .

And when you see clouds

Upon the hills,

You soon will see crowds of daffodils . . .

The shower passed on to the hills, the train to the plains. The sun came out and the clouds rolled by, and a rainbow lit up the sky.

ACKNOWLEDGEMENTS

The author wishes to thank Sohini Mitra and Kankana Basu for helping put this memoir into shape, and Mihir Joglekar for his lively and evocative illustrations.

PRAISE FOR THE BOOK

'It's a story plump with joy, tenderness, and sadness. In many ways, this is a precursor to his books, a window into some of his formative years that shaped [his] writing'—*The Hindu*

'An extraordinary offering by India's most loved author, the book captures the little nuances—fantasies, expectations and often the void—that children face but their guardians don't know about. The book has been beautifully illustrated by Mihir Joglekar'—*Hindustan Times*

'Bond deftly gives us a peek into the Delhi of 1940s . . . Bond is not sceptical of his readers judging him. He keeps the simplicity intact . . . such candour wins our hearts and compels us to read on as his friend. *Looking for the Rainbow* is a fine balance of enthusiasm, innocence, pain, loss and grief'—*Asian Age*

'Gorgeously illustrated, the charming Mr Bond's poignant prose makes *Looking for the Rainbow* a must-read for both children and adults'—*Live Mint*

Looking for the Rainbow

My Years with Daddy

'When we are small we need someone to hold our hand in the dark.'

At age eight, Ruskin escapes his jail-like boarding school in the hills and goes to live with his father in Delhi. His time in the capital is filled with books, visits to the cinema, music, and walks and conversations with his father—a dream life for a curious and wildly imaginative boy, which turns tragic all too soon.

For years, Ruskin Bond has regaled and mesmerized readers with his tales. In *Looking for the Rainbow*, Bond travels to his past, recalling his favourite adventures (and misadventures) with extraordinary charm, sprinklings of wit, a pinch of poignance and not a trace of bitterness.

What you're holding, dear reader, is a classic in the making.

Dust on the Mountain

'The hill station, with all its glitter, was just a pretty gift box with nothing inside.'

When twelve-year-old Bisnu decides to go to Mussoorie to earn for his family, he has no idea how dangerous and lonely life in a town can be for a boy on his own.

As he sets out to work on the limestone quarries, with the choking dust enveloping the beautiful mountain air, he finds that he longs for his little village in the Himalayas.

Anitha Balachandran's illustrations add a bright splash of colour to one of Ruskin Bond's most memorable stories.

Cricket for the Crocodile

'Nakoo got his teeth deep into the cricket ball and chewed. Revenge was sweet.'

Ranji's team finds an unexpected opponent—a nosy crocodile—when it plays a cricket match against the village boys. Annoyed at the swarm of boys crowding the riverbank and the alarming cricket balls plopping around his place of rest, Nakoo the crocodile decides to take his revenge.

This sumptuously illustrated edition brings alive yet another one of Ruskin Bond's delightful tales.

The Day Grandfather Tickled a Tiger

A heart-warming story of love and friendship

When Grandfather discovers a little tiger cub on a hunting expedition, he decides to take it home. Christened Timothy, the cub grows up as any regular house pet, with a monkey and a mongrel for company. But as he grows older, Timothy starts behaving strangely, and Grandfather decides that it's time to send him away.

This sumptuously illustrated edition brings to life one of Bond's most captivating stories.

The Tree Lover

Everything that you've always loved about Ruskin Bond is back

His mesmerizing descriptions of nature and his wonderful way with words—this is Ruskin Bond at his finest.

Read on as Rusty tells the story of his grandfather's relationship with the trees around him, and how he is convinced that they love him back with as much tenderness as he showers on them.

This beautifully illustrated edition brings to life one of Bond's most enduring tales and is sure to win over yet another generation of readers.